The Cat Who Said His Bedtime Prayers

AMY MORTON

LifeRich Publishing is a registered trademark of The Reader's Digest Association, Inc.

LifeRich Publishing books may be ordered through booksellers or by contacting:

LifeRich Publishing
1663 Liberty Drive
Bloomington, IN 47403
www.liferichpublishing.com
844-686-9607

ISBN: 978-1-4897-3865-3 (sc)
ISBN: 978-1-4897-3864-6 (hc)
ISBN: 978-1-4897-3866-0 (e)

Print information available on the last page.

LifeRich Publishing rev. date: 12/13/2021

The Cat Who Said His Bedtime Prayers

A golden cat prances through the tall grass in front of a yellow house at the end of a long boulevard. On each side of the boulevard, daffodils and tulips stand tall with colorful petals on top. Tree buds burst with small leaves on their outstretched branches and birds sing as they gather twigs to make nests. Nature wears springtime like a magnificent crown—a testimony to the King of Kings that Jesus makes all things new and beautiful.

Michael was walking down the boulevard away from his house when Morris, his cat with thick golden fur and brilliant blue eyes, caught up to him. Michael reached down and scratched him under the chin. "Good—bye kitty!" Michael was on spring break, heading to his friend's house for the weekend. Morris brushed against his leg, but then he saw a bird and pounced off after it.

Michael arrived at John's house. John and his dad, Pastor Dustin, were playing basketball. John's dad saw Michael and passed him the ball, then he excused himself from the game. He left so he could prepare for tomorrow's Easter service. Every time Michael stayed at John's house, they would go to church the next day.

The next morning at church, the teacher explained that Jesus is the one and only perfect Son of God. For when he died on the cross and rose again, everyone was forgiven for their sins and given the gift of eternal life! The teacher looked around the classroom and said, "All you have to do is confess with your mouth that Jesus is Lord, and believe in your heart that God raised him from the dead. Then you will be saved." He paused for a moment. "Does anyone believe this?" asked the teacher. Michael quickly raised his hand. Then others followed. Michael raised his hand every Easter because he thought this was the best news ever!

John's parents brought Michael home after church. Michael saw Morris playing outside with the birds. He was lying in the tall grass, waiting patiently for birds to land near him so he could pounce on them. Morris didn't catch any birds, but it sure was fun to watch!

After a while Michael called Morris over to the porch where he was sitting. "Here, Morris. Here, kitty—kitty!" he yelled. Morris came running—he's an obedient cat. Morris rubbed his face and side against Michael, who in turn scratched him under the chin. Morris began purring like a motorboat. He was the happiest cat whenever he was scratched under the chin.

Michael told Morris what he learned at church. Morris's ears perked up as he listened to what Michael called "the best news ever!" So Michael told him about Jesus and eternal life in heaven. Morris always seemed to understand. Michael told him everything he learned, then gently tossed him over his shoulder and carried him into the house.

Michael went to sit down for lunch with his parents and sister. They talked about the best news ever and laughed about Morris trying to catch birds. After lunch, Michael's dad, Robert, announced that there were a dozen eggs hidden in the house. He and his sister were to find them! Robert set the timer, and they were off to the races! They looked in every nook and cranny until every last egg was found. The eggs really were hidden treasures because each one had a gift inside!

At the end of the game, Robert said, "This game is a good way to remember that although you can't see Jesus, he left his holy spirit to live in your heart. Just like hidden treasure, the Holy Spirit is there to help you." *Wow,* thought Michael, *more good news!*

Michael had a fun-filled day, and at last it was time for bed. Every night Morris curled up at the end of his bed, and then it was time to say their prayers. Michael had said his prayers at bedtime since he was five years old. That's when his dad taught him how to pray. So Michael taught Morris how to pray too. Morris and Michael always said their bedtime prayers together.

One day Morris was moving very slowly. It was clear he wasn't well. Michael's parents took him to the veterinarian, and they learned he would not be able to heal. Michael spent extra time with him after that, petting him gently to help him feel better. He told Morris how much he loved him, how much God loved him, and all about heaven. Michael explained that in heaven he would have no pain. He would be so happy! And one day, Michael would be there to rub him under his chin again.

Morris passed on to heaven a few months after that, and Michael and his family were sad. Michael cried because he could no longer talk to Morris, pet him, or watch him chase birds. He was sad because Morris no longer curled up at the foot of his bed every night, but he remembered what his dad had said about the Holy Spirit living in his heart to help him. So when Michael said his bedtime prayers, he let God know how much he missed his kitty, and he thanked God for the time they had together. Michael felt better after prayer because he knew God was listening.

As time passed, Michael was comforted by the Holy Spirit over the loss of Morris. He was reassured that one day he would see him again because heaven is where all believers go—even Morris the cat, whose ears perked up when he heard the best news ever; the cat who said his bedtime prayers.

The wolf shall dwell with the lamb, and the leopard shall lie down with the young goat, and the calf and the lion and the fattened calf together; and a little child shall lead them. (Isaiah 11:6—9)